"Dreaming On"
The Collection

18 Short Stories
with Illustrations

by
John Emery and Jeff Markham

Bloomington, IN  Milton Keynes, UK

authorHOUSE®

AuthorHouse™
1663 Liberty Drive, Suite 200
Bloomington, IN 47403
www.authorhouse.com
Phone: 1-800-839-8640

AuthorHouse™ UK Ltd.
500 Avebury Boulevard
Central Milton Keynes, MK9 2BE
www.authorhouse.co.uk
Phone: 08001974150

This book is a work of fiction. People, places, events, and situations are the product of the author's imagination. Any resemblance to actual persons, living or dead, or historical events, is purely coincidental.

First published by AuthorHouse 9/20/2006

ISBN: 1-4259-5542-8 (sc)

Printed in the United States of America
Bloomington, Indiana

This book is printed on acid-free paper.

TABLE OF CONTENTS

COMPLIMENTS TO THE CHEF!
STORY OF JOANNA

by John Emery

There he was sitting on board an Air Canada jet heading for Toronto.

It seemed only five minutes ago that he walked into a London wine bar one October evening with his musical chum Brady.

The sound of piano and double bass greeted them as they walked in; this cheered the two guys up no end as Brady was a classic rock musician. He was an original punk having played with Reckless Eric and most of that wild band of scallywags. Brady had a great aura about him and was a great partner to have when visiting any London wine bar.

Sitting strategically on a stool in the distant corner sat a blonde chanteuse surrounded by five vibrant friends. They pumped out a lot of hot estrogen between them creating some mayhem in the male dominated hostelry.

"Are you Austrian" was his pitch as he approached her with verve. "No I am from Canada and so are all the girls."

She was the type of magnet that girls must place in the centre not necessarily to attract or divert attention but in a position so that she can check and assess all incoming traffic.

If the guy was good he would be guaranteed an introduction to all the other girls. If not he would be told to go away.

She was a sort of concierge for all her mates though she was very beautiful in her own right, long legs, blonde tousled hair that fell over her shoulders and an indication that she came from the higher echelons of Canadian society.

I believe Celine Dion is about to become President he said casually to Marina. That was her name.

"I sincerely hope not" she smiled.

He began to feel what is known as "Wine bar relaxed" a situation created by the very environment and surroundings.

Even then he had no idea that in the midst of the company was an Exocet missile which was about to explode and have the desired effect on the opposite sex!

She had her back to him with the other girls until she decided to turn around.

Equipped with big saucer like eyes, and short dark hair plus a smile that would sink a battleship she was 5 foot 4 inches of pure magnificence. The fact that she had beautiful breasts could only add to the finished product.

His panache and smooth skills- if ever they were there at all flew out of the Window and out came the immortal words "Compliments to the Chef."

He moved closer to the young lady shaped like a Pocket Venus and she smiled.

Within inches of her beautiful frame he hollered like a man in pain "Compliments to the chef. You remind me of Barbara Hershey."

"Really" she smiled politely.

"I think the chef is off duty. He is in the corner so if you want a ham sandwich you had better speak to him before he goes."

Totally ignoring her speech he said "I used to have girlfriends like you when I was 19. They were fabulous, what do I actually have to do to chat you up?"

"Is it true that Girls Just Wanna Have Fun."

"They do" said Joanna who was an interior designer. He then burst into the first verse of the Cyndi Lauper song with great enthusiasm at which point she collapsed with laughter.

She was seriously trying to work out whether this guy was mad or not, he couldn't be drunk because it was too early.

But she was a girl on holiday for heaven's sake and no approach had been made all evening. So she thought he was original if nothing else.

"What's the thing about the chef" she asked her new suitor. "Oh well it's simply that whoever concocted you - you know put the recipe together - got it right."

"Oh I see" she nodded.

"I would also say that inch for inch and pound for pound you are the female equivalent of Sugar Ray Leonard."

"You think I look like a boxer? How dare you I've never been so insulted. I think you should see a doctor. You are seriously ill."

"I have had some unusual chat up lines in my time but never quite like this."

"Just for the record my mum and dad concocted me as you so delicately put it and I don't think they see me in that light at all,"

He looked at her and gave her a cuddle. That was the first thing he did that she liked.

Joanna was her name and he knew that she was special...

He could see it quite early. He could talk to her and have a laugh with her. Where had she been all his life?

No wonder he was on the plane.

He had decided to jet across the Atlantic from one side of the world to the other with the required documents in order to put his hands firmly on her shoulder and "Personally Arrest" his Little Mountie.

She was to find herself at the top of his menu under the title of "Special Lumberjack Omelet" with the required grated cheese, and relevant spices and flavoring. To be eaten and digested with no clothes on.

Instant Surrender
Story of Talia

by John Emery

A man can experience many rebuffs and rejections in his life but one that must surely take the biscuit is to be turned down on the grounds of having to report for Army duty. But so it was with Talia.

She was leggy with long blonde flowing hair and appeared to have stepped right off the cover of Vogue or Harpers Bazaar. And yet she was sitting at a table all on her own. A bit like a wall flower.

He looked across at her from a distance and assessed the situation. After all he was in the Company of Wolves, a male bastion of ravers out for a good time. So it was wise to tread gently.

Talia's sister sat opposite her with her boyfriend covering Talia as though she were a "Protected species" not to be touched. Yet, Talia, still looked very much alone.

Often a person can create their very own aura by just being on their own. Even if they are protected on all flanks they still look vunerable.

This vibe will always bring the man out in every man no matter who he is. He instantly wants to protect her.

Protect her from what? The world, the club, maybe he even wants to protect her from himself.

He eventually descended on the table like an eagle swooping for its prey. The Latin music boomed out and everyone was dancing. Yet he didn't want to ask her for a dance. He wanted to talk to her and to get to know her.

So after one whole hour he made his way to her table and asked her politely if she would like a drink. She nodded quietly and smiled as he sat down next to her. It was table service so this was acceptable.

He spoke to her elder sister and boyfriend who were both charming. He felt he needed their permission to continue any dalliance with the young beauty.

He was to discover the sheer depth of her character as the evening wore on. Her name was Tally which puzzled him. But nevertheless he proceeded to do his Woody Allen pitch- a good old nutmeg based on an ordinary guy trying to get off with a beautiful woman.

Sometimes it worked. Sometimes it didn't.

She continued to laugh and smile and they came to an agreement as to what she would like to drink or rather what the table would like to drink.

The order was to be made from a menu. This was not the Dog & Duck in Peckham High Street, so one had to behave accordingly.

The fascination of her very name, "Tally" hypnotized him until he worked out that it had to be short for Talia as in Talia Shire, a well known actress who played in the Godfather Trilogy and the Rocky films.

She ordered with her sister a very strange drink that he had never heard of. A cocktail with a bizarre spelling. It arrived in a type of carafe.

"Do you want one?" said her sister. "Is there enough?" he said. She passed him a small container of the liquid. It was similar to rocket fuel.

Talia and her sister came from Israel and were here on holiday. First thought was to get her to the theatre. That was always a good ruse. Test of character also as to whether she could handle a good evening of Shakespeare.

Also a touch of the "was she only a pretty face?" assessment. One evening at the theatre followed by dinner can tell a man all he needs to know about a woman. Plenty of time for chat and negotiation plus supreme entertainment culminating in a fine selection of the best food in town.

Also the opportunity to see her right home to her door would present itself.

Everything was moving along smoothly until she delivered the most original punch line in the history of dating.

"I won't be able to go to the theatre with you as I have been called up by the Israeli Army. It is compulsory so I have no choice."

The very thought of her dressed in a khaki outfit covered in mottled camouflage was enough to drive him crazy. What on earth it would do to the enemy he dreaded to guess.

So it was very much "Tally ho" to Tally as she set off for the dusty plains of Israel, set for a kibbutz lifestyle and some hard graft for one year.

Would she ever be the same again? He thought as he watched her bum wiggle in front him as she attacked the Cuban dance floor with verge and energy.

"Come and have a dance" she said to him.

Normally he would but not this time "I'm fine" he said. He would prefer to sit down and watch this unique vision of a young girl at her peak, wiggle her hips, throw her head back in defiance and dance with her sister.

He could see her now in full battle dress in the Israeli Army and had one simple message for the enemy "INSTANT SURRENDER."

Carry On Nurse
The story of Ivana

By John Emery

A film such as Carry on Nurse and Carry on Doctor has encouraged every male patient to believe that all nurses are "Hot stuff". But is it the uniform that makes them so attractive or is it the woman inside the tight fitting sky blue outfit that is the attraction.

Women love men in a uniform and it is the same the other way round. There is nothing sexier than a nurse "dressed up in sky blue" showing order and discipline. It will soon knock any man into shape. Your average male patient will go into a hospital full of top medical equipment and he will not be impressed at all. When introduced to a high flying consultant he will have two things on his mind (1) Please Fix It and (2) When can I go home.

But if you put a nurse at the end of his bed he will soon pay attention.

If she tells him what is wrong with him – he will listen. And if she tells him to jump in the lake, he will also listen. He may decide not to jump into the lake but he will listen.

Their trick is simply, how to grasp a guy's attention span, a skill at which they are past masters at. For them it's a bit like "Going fishing" or "Falling off a log" like the words in the song "Its second nature to me now – like breathing out and breathing in…"

She can spot a specific patient in a ward, clock onto him and cure him so quickly it is untrue. All she needs to do is stand at the end of his bed. After that he stands no chance at all.

The next thing you know he is out of bed and in the Admin area checking the roster to see what time she is due on next.

"I thought you had a broken arm", the Matron will say, "Oh no I'm fine thank you. I was just checking what time my nurse is next on duty".

This is all very encouraging but why is he behaving like this? Simply because his mind is not on the illness at all - his mind is on the nurse.

When the "Mix" works it is fantastic. When the patient really does love the nurse and she feels the same it is awesome! But it is also very rare!!

And so it was with Ivana the nurse on the 9th floor she was the "Blonde Bombshell" from Slovakia who was terrific and five days under her spell was enough for him to quickly get well. But although he recovered from the fracture he found it difficult to recover from her.

Her only problem seemed to be her liking for country music. She had to be joking!! No one in their right mind could surely like country music he thought. God she is in a bad way.

"Oh she fixed my broken arm so I can fix her broken heart." How corny can you get? Surely Ivana couldn't like songs like that. She definitely needed some repair work done on her choice of music.

After all she was built like a "Pocket Battleship" such as Potemkin but was much prettier!! She would take hold of him in search of his temperature with her right hand while holding a stop watch in her left. She could have been the Olympic coach for the Ukraine Athletics team.

She was efficient, precise, and good at her job and worked four days a week doing 12 hour shifts. She set a great example so he knew that he would ALWAYS want to look fit, strong and healthy when she was around.

"What's the matter with your shirts? Why don't you wash them," she said. "I am looking for a good woman," he would say to her. "Well if you find her and she really is a good woman she is not going to wash your shirts is she?"

She had him on the run and he loved it.

The first thing he wanted to do was kiss her and squeeze her. But he thought that might not be a good idea. People might get the wrong impression.

The irony is that when a guy goes into hospital he doesn't really want to be there. But after a few days you can't get rid of him.

And even when he is better, he will still come back and haunt you. And so it was with him.

"Ivana – will you please let me take you out to dinner?" he said handing her an ENORMOUS box of chocolates.

"No. It is very unprofessional. Also I can see clearly that you have not washed your shirt." He was tempted to ask for his chocolates back but he thought that would be childish.

"I am married," she told him. "Where's your ring then," he chipped in brightly. "Mind your own business" she told him.

How do I get rid of this guy she thought? There was nothing in her coaching manual that covered this area.

Having popped in to say hello at a later date he thought he saw a small light at the end of the tunnel.

"I have had my haircut," she told him. "Really," he said. "Do you like it" she asked.

He nodded in agreement for it was her crowning glory after all and she did look very much like Goldie Hawn! Also the fact that she wanted his opinion on her haircut indicated that he was making progress.

Following this he discovered the word LASKA which was Slovak for Love. He found the word in a dictionary.

So finally, the question is what was an experienced journalist doing on all fours wading through Czech/Slovak dictionaries trying to learn "Fluent Slovak?"

What he really wanted was a particular phrase and he felt if it took forever he would find it.

One rainy day he got lucky he came across the phrase he was looking for, KOCHAM CIEBIE, which pronounced correctly was CORE HAM SHE EB BE.

What does this phrase mean? The journalist and the nurse knows so what will happen next?

Heaven knows but a beautiful girl always wins the heart of any man!!

Hula Hoops
USA Style
The story of Viviana

by John Emery

It is common knowledge that a woman is never allowed into a man's club, it is the one bastion of "retreat" he has left and will guard it for all it is worth, unless she is wearing a hula-hooped jumper that is.

He wandered in the lounge bar of his club and could not help noticing the sight of hoops in the corner. Round and round they went hypnotizing him until he could no longer resist.

He approached slowly and sat down next to them. What he had failed to notice was that inside the hooped jumper was a lovely young lady. She really shouldn't have been in the club at all but he didn't seem bothered.

"Do you mind if I sit here" he asked the hoops. "No feel free" was his reply. His head continued to spin as he glared at the jumper guarding and protecting the two large breasts inside.

He mumbled the word "Fascinating."

"Can I help you at all" said the young lady inside the jumper" "I beg your pardon I was admiring your jumper. Would you like a drink?"

She agreed and he returned with a bottle of wine.

He wasted no time. "What you should do" he advised her, "is wear a black one on a Monday with white hoops; a green one on a Tuesday with yellow hoops; a brown one on a Wednesday with white hoops; a red one on a Thursday with blue hoops; and on Friday wear a pure white sweater with one black hoop around the middle."

"Do you think so" she asked.

"Yes I do" he replied.

He assured her that he was absolutely sure of it and was very surprised when she told him that she worked in the fashion industry and knew exactly how to dress without his help.

Taking into account his fashion rota she asked, "What then do you think I should wear at the weekends."

He assured her that was not important for she would have pulled so many men during the week that she would have to spend the entire weekend trying to fend them off.

You seem to know all the answers she said to him.

"No I just know that men like hula-hooped jumpers very much. Wrapped in such a garment on a regular basis you would be irresistible to the opposite sex and they would be putty in your hands".

"How do you know that's what I want" she interjected…

"Well you are in a men's club aren't you. You are obviously not here to play snooker or billiards."

They laughed and joked for twenty minutes or so and he still had not even asked her name. As they became more and more intoxicated she began to smile and asked him, "Where is my Dion & The Belmonts CD."

He seemed at odds with this question.

What do you mean?

"You chatted me up exactly a year ago and promised me a classic Dion & the Belmonts CD, a trip to Austria, lunch at the Savoy and a million other things. The only way to trace you was to find out the name of your club."

"Were you wearing a hooped jumper at the time" he asked her. "What's that got to do with it?" she hollered.

"If you weren't wearing a hooped jumper I obviously cannot remember you." This infuriated the girl and the hoops as well.

They began throbbing and vibrating in a dangerous manner.

"If you don't calm down you will explode out of your lovely jumper."

"Sod my jumper" she screamed "You are avoiding the question and missing the point. Do you normally chat up girls and then fail to contact them as promised?"

He explained that he must have had a computer breakdown and could not send the required e-mails as promised.

He slowly moved to the bar to order another bottle of wine for the two of them. As he sat down on his return he grinned at her.

"What are you laughing at" she snarled at him.

"I know exactly who you are. You are Viviana from New York. That's Vivien with an A at the end. Is that correct?"

She nodded in the direction of yes.

He put his arm around her and thanked her for tracking him down. He said the reason he really did not try harder to keep in touch with her was that she seemed to show very little interest at the time.

"Well actually I had a cold and was not in the mood."

"Well you should have worn a very large woolen jumper shouldn't you," he stated "Preferably with hoops on to keep you warm."

She slapped him round the face and they kissed.

PROTECTED SPECIES

By John Emery

The female of the species is deadlier than the male, according to a lovely little song by the band SPACE. A "protected species" however is something that needs to be looked after and nurtured and who better to do that than a man?

Girls may have their filo fax: credit cards: designer suits and all the trimmings but they still need a man to tell them how good they look: how fantastic they are: and also how desirable. Is there no admiration. What is the point?

But what happens when a young filly makes her debut on her first Holiday outing and is guaranteed "protection" from five friends who batten down the hatches so firmly it has the opposite effect.

It is off putting to young admirers but not those who know no boundaries and are very determined.

"Can I speak to your friend" is the opening gambit, the concierge explained that "It is her first holiday and we are looking after her. You can buy her lemonade if you want but that's all."

It may be her first holiday but they have under-rated the youngest member of their fraternity.

Passing her a glass of lemonade he says to the young filly "you remind me of Tess of the D'Urbervilles," winking to her in the process and also trying to get across the fact that he was well read. There is little response but the connection has been made.

He trots off to the book shop returning with a copy of TESS by Thomas Hardy. Writing a personal inscription inside the cover. He hands it to her. She responds with a smile for this is the first present ever given to her by a total stranger.

She reads the book with passion and is absent for the next two nights.

While her friends are out on the town, she is in her hotel room fascinated by the book.

"Where is my little friend" asked the admirer. The concierge informs him that she is back at the hotel reading the book.

The intention of the present was to cheer her up, not have her locked away in a stuffy hotel room. So he went off to the market to buy some strawberries.

He made his way to the hotel in which she was staying. He knew the room number and on his way up popped into the kitchen to borrow some white overalls.

His knock on the door was greeted with an invitation to come in. "I knew you would come" she said. "Please sit down. I have nearly finished the book."

"Those strawberries are for me I presume"

He nodded. "Well you realize I can't eat then don't you."

"Now why would that be," he asked the young lady." Well according to the book the strawberries given to TESS lead to her downfall. Now you don't want that to happen to me do you: I have grown to love this book and I treasure the story…"

How old are you he asked his little friend.

"I am 17" she said. "Are you really" he replied.

"You want to deflower me don't you. Just like the book. He smiled in the direction of her yes.

"Are you a nice man" she asked. "No I am not a nice man he replied."

"At least you're honest" she said locking the door.

Before seducing him...

WINNER TAKES IT ALL
The story of Emmanuelle

By John Emery

Sylvia Kristel became very famous playing the role of Emmanuelle on screen during the seventies and left a legacy of "sex symbols" in her trail as she bowed out gracefully.

Following Bardot she was probably the sexiest actress ever to appear on the screen. She made three films (Emmanuelle 1, 2 & 3) and then disappeared.

But even she would have found it difficult to compete with the girls today for she was "simply a figment of every man's imagination" and not for real.

Well that's what he thought anyway when he walked into a West London Singles bar and saw the "Real Thing" sitting there.

The words "Vive Le Difference" screamed out as she simply sat poised on top of a bar stool.

This was play on words from Casablanca "Of all the bars in the entire world I had to walk into yours…"

For he was about to play a dangerous game and he would live to regret it.

Emmanuelle worked there as a waitress and it was her job to be friendly.

He knew she was French and he wanted to take part in the game. That was what it was about to become, a game and a battle of wills.

The French Woman within her own culture is Queen of the Chessboard. She is taught from an early age to pout, act like a spoiled child, slam doors and be provocative to gain the attention of man.

She knows that she is the prize so if any man wanted to win her he had to work very hard at it! He had read this in a book so he was ready to do battle!!!

Any French girl to any English man is very sexy. It is automatic. He was instantly intoxicated by her and was like a "magnet" with a desire to attach itself to her body.

She whispered in his ear "It's a nice day today yes?" He responded in a state of rapture in a desperate bid to communicate. His attempt at conversation was a cross between Ispector Clouseau and Marcel Marceau!

But he persevered and asked the young lady if he could buy her a drink. She said yes. "I would like a large scotch and cake" she said and he laughed "I didn't realize you were an alcoholic!" She looked at him unmoved.

"I have very expensive tastes" she ignored him. "But you know... If you can't afford it,"

"No I was only joking" he blustered.

He discovered that she came from Brittany in France "You will not find it on the map" she informed him.

"Why" he asked.

"Because the correct spelling is, Bretagne."

She wafted the drink down and said she would like another one. He was surprised at the speed of her alcoholic consumption. She obviously had a strong constitution...

He waved his arms in the air declaring the phrase "Je le ne regriette rienne" the title of an Edith Piaf song. It was the only French he knew so he had to use it.

"You don't mind buying me another drink"

He waved his arms in the air. "What the hell. Let's go for it. You think my French is good?" he added.

"I think your French is fantastic" she smiled. "In fact I would say it's outstanding. What do you do – I am interested."

He explained that he was a writer and his subject was mainly theatre. He asked her if her name was really Emmanuelle – and connected in any way with the film of the same name.

"I have never heard of her" she said shrugging her shoulders. He told her that he was surprised that she was not aware of it.

"Well you are obviously much older than me," she said by way of a put down. The game was on.

"What a beautiful name Emmanuelle is…"

She nodded in approval "your French is getting better monsieur"

Ordering a third scotch and coke at the bar.

Eager to continue this rendezvous he said smoothly "I take you to a club – yes."

"You take me to a club – no." she replied.

She explained that her English was not very good but it was much better than his French.

At this point he was struggling and as the evening wore on they continued to exchange English and French phrases by way of conversation.

She thought he was a bit odd actually but definitely less predictable than the others. He was also not rude. Not deliberately so anyway.

He then began to throw in lots of "song titles" such as My Cherie Amour, Cest si Bon and chanso L 'amour in a desperate bid to impress her. He even added a chorus of Les Bicycles des Belsize for good measure.

"Trebien" he whispered in her ear. "What is Trebien" she smiled in response.

"You are Trebien Emmanuelle. That means good doesn't it. And you are good. You are very good."

She burst out laughing at his "Dreadful French" She thought her English was bad. But his French was worse.

She fully expected him to turn into inspector Clouseau any moment. And he would have if it was absolutely necessary.

But the moment of truth was about to arrive in the shape of a bill. The scotch and cokes had mounted up throughout the evening and he had joined with her in her sublime choice of tipple.

The combined total of drinks consumed outweighed the power of his credit card and at wine bar prices he was definitely in a pickle. The bill was enormous and much to his surprise Miss Bretagne paid it for him.

He was very embarrassed but it was OK.

She then took him home by taxi and made passionate love on the floor with him… "I want you to have lots of je t'aime with me" she demanded.

He couldn't believe his luck. There was a beautiful French girl on top of him – and she had also paid the bill.

He would definitely return to the wine bar again if this was the type of thing that happened.

"Why are you making love to me?" he smiled.

"Because I like you" she said.

But what he had forgotten was that she was Queen of the Chessboard and she had yet to make her final move.

She whispered in his ear "You must go now."

He reacted in disbelief. "You want me to go now?

"I must go to bed." Said Emmanuelle. "I am working tomorrow. Please close the door on your way out."

He never saw her again.

The moral of this story is never mess around with a French girl because you will never win. She has you covered from every angle.

Winner takes It All!

PUMP ACTION

By John Emery

He had decided that he was now without question the greatest "sexual athlete" this side of Crewe Junction. Of this there was no doubt.

It had taken him 20 Clear years to get to this point in terms of his masculinity – after major rejection from his first girlfriend. It had worked in his favor but only after a lot of hard work.

He started to go swimming in the mornings, running in the afternoons and making love to a "blow up doll" in the evenings – "honing" his equipment to face the biggest of challenges: that of satisfying a woman.

His last exercise in this department was a total disaster. He was on top of his last girlfriend giving his all when she said to him "What actually are you doing."

He was pounding away and he could not believe the response. "I have bad news for you matey you are doing it wrong. You do not turn me on at all" at which point she got up and left leaving him in one hell of a quandary.

The hardest point of a man's ego is his sexual prowess. To hit him there is where it hurts.

He had caressed her body and produced his manhood at the required time and inserted it just where it said on the diagram. But she still wasn't happy. He was using the popular "Pump Action" method and could not see where he had possibly gone wrong. As she left the flat she said, "You really do not have a clue do you?"

He asked her for fresh instructions and a new diagram and she just shook her head. No chance. You will have to find out for yourself. You need a lot more practice. "The clue is to find the G spots." she said. "That's the key."

"G spots" he said "What the hell are they. You don't have a map with you at all. I need some directions here…

She smiled at his sarcasm. "You think to laugh at it the problem will go away. Well it won't and I will now leave you to it. The word "Goodbye" rang in his head as she slammed the door.

He was very hurt. He felt like a World War 11 pilot having been shot down in flames. He had never been so insulted and had never been so damaged in his entire life.

How could she hurt him so? She was a Modern Young Woman but surely they were not supposed to go around insulting people.

Not to be outdone he whizzed down to the library and asked for a book on G spots. The young lady at the library looked at him quizzically. He asked for a book with illustrations covering all the G spots.

The librarian said "Do you mean a lady's G spots."

"Yes he answered proudly." She looked at him in a quizzical fashion. She felt there was no such book available to her knowledge but she really liked his honesty.

"What actually is the problem" she asked in true customer service fashion.

He told her his problem and she promptly invited him round for the evening and said she would give him a personal lesson that would set him up for life.

She informed him that she knew where all the spots were and he would not need a book. She explained that she would be happy to help him in any way that she could.

"Kiss me on the knee" she said firmly. "Are you sure" he said "Yes I am sure" she smiled.

"Qooh sensational" she cried.

"Is that good" he asked.

"Fantastic, do it again, this time on the other knee."

She then asked him to take all his clothes off. He took all his cloths off and she couldn't believe her luck

He was built like a stallion.

"Listen touch me where no man has ever touched me before "Where actually is that" he asked. "I don't know" she said. He began to stroke her cheek and blow in her left ears' and she promptly hit the ceiling!

"Blow in the right ear as well."

She then went into the kitchen and produced a frying pan. "Hit me on the head with that." She said. "Are you joking" he asked. "Do it" she said and he did. He hit her on the head with the frying pan – but did so very gently.

"What shall we do next" he asked her.

There was a scream of delight. "Is your head one of your G spots do you think." He asked her eagerly. "I don't know" she said crashing to the floor with laughter – realizing that she had never had such fun in her life.

"Make love to my arm," she asked and he did. He caressed her arm in such a gentle manner that it triggered an enormous orgasm which came from nowhere.

She wriggled on the floor in some kind of pain and he held her to make sure she was ok. "Make love to me now" she demanded. Can I use my pump action method?" he asked.

"Use whatever method you like" she hollered.

He made love in an ordinary manner and she thought it was fantastic. Following this she jumped up and asked him to put his clothes on.

"Get dressed – I'm going to make you some dinner."

"What about the G spots" he asked her.

"I wouldn't worry about that –

"You are my G spot."

"Whoever filled you with such rubbish needs her head examined…

And yes they did live happily ever after.

An Email Called Lydia

By John Emery

Man constantly chasing woman with the old A and B equation. It is simply based on two girls, the pretty one and her friend.

Girl B would be the strong one of the two who has kept the friendship ticking over throughout the years. Also Girl B is a girl who never did get the recognition that she deserved.

She is used to sitting down and listening to stories of the other one's constant parade of boyfriends and how difficult it was for her friend to keep turning them away.

"How do you do it" Girl B would ask.

Throwing her head back Miss A would say "Oh Lydia you know what it's like. They just keep ringing me up. I had to turn a guy down the other day and on reflection I didn't even know who it was."

"But how did he get your phone number then" asked Miss B, "Oh the guys just pass it round. You know what men are like."

"But he could have been really nice" said Girl B "You should have given him my number." Miss A shrugged the matter aside. It was of no importance to a girl with an address book full of admirers.

Girl B was used to carrying along a conversation while her glamorous friend just sat posing and preening. But she didn't mind as it had always been this way ever since they were at school together.

On first viewing, all he saw was her back. Having spotted Miss Glamorous at the side of the swimming pool, he moved over like a rocket. This was mainly because Girl A was wearing a bikini that was barely covering her body.

In contrast Girl B sat wearing a one-piece costume in dark blue. She was "the friend" and all glamorous girls had one of these.

Girl B was slightly tubby and her hair was distraught, looking as though a bomb had hit it. But she was very friendly and during the course of one hour all the conversation was with her.

The more he spoke to her the more he got to like her he could see that deep down she was a very attractive woman.

She had to be married but he decided that didn't matter. They were getting on really well and they decided to exchange e-mail addresses.

What clichéd his first reaction was the title of her e-mail box which was Lydia Gravy. He thought that was very witty and an accurate reflection of her as a person.

She was after all the one who came up to him at the bar while he was ordering the drinks to deliver the fatal message. "Sorry – she is not interested. She has declined your invitation to dinner…"

"Oh well" he said glancing closely at her. He noticed that standing next to him she was very petite. She looked prettier standing up than sitting down.

His brain (the one in his head and not in his trousers) began slowly to work. "Do you have to go" he asked her.

She nodded heading in pursuit of her pretty friend saying casually "Don't forget to e-mail me."

And e-mail he did bombarding the airways with loads of messages. First one asked how her lovely friend was plus the fact that he had forgotten her name in the process.

His first e-mail was a great success. He used his wilt and skill by ending it with the classic phrase," please give my best wishes to Mr. Gravy."

The reply was interesting. The message read: "The kids are fine. But there is no Mr. Gravy."

The plot began to thicken.

Was he ready to undertake a relationship with Lydia Gravy and two children?

It would mean that he would have to take her to Bond Street to get her hair cut and also to Miss Selfridges for a new swimming costume.

But bugger the expense he thought.

Anyone with a name such as Lydia Gravy had to be given some serious consideration.

End of story

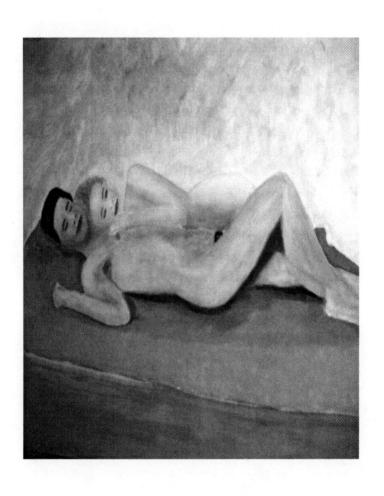

HONEY IS THAT YOU

By John Emery

The words rang in his head "Nadeeen – Honey is that you" and it had absolutely nothing to do with Chuck Berry at all. He had seen a very attractive girl but the circumstances were very difficult.

She was inches away from him which was very good but also inches away were both her father and mother. So he had to think quickly or to quote a current trend "he had to think on his feet."

Here we had a guy who had to be taken seriously. He was definitely a contender for he had his own computer and printer and parked outside the house was his own BSA bike. This guy was definitely a catch in his own right for any girl.

But then again the girl herself was terrific.

He thought she would fit very nicely on the back of his BSA bike doing his general "image" no harm at all.

The opportunity was there for him so he had to grab it. "Do you have your own website" he asked the gorgeous young lady who had decided to sit down and relax. "I do not have my own website but I am seriously thinking of getting one" she replied.

"Oh good" said the young man nonchalantly.

This was the closest thing to crazy he had ever been and it was also a test of his character as to how he would handle it. The question is basically what happens to a guy when the most beautiful girl in the world happens to be inches away from him. What does he do next?

It's a good question but also a tricky one for on one side it was her mum and the other side her father.

He could of course do the Duck Walk across the carpet or swing his arms in an "Air Guitar" style but that would not be recommended.

Nadeeen sat strong and being fully aware of the situation and the guy's distress came to the rescue – as young ladies do – and asked if he would like a cup of tea.

"I would like one of those" he replied looking very casual. "Two sugars or three" asked Nadeeen.

"Well" he replied shrugging his shoulders. "I'm easy you know, two, three, or four sugars, I can handle it. I'll leave it up to you, looking so casual that he proceeded to fall backwards over the chair!

There was an almighty crash, as he found himself flat out on the carpet, but he had to carry on because that's what men did. They must continue to go forward regardless of the situation. Falling backwards from the chair, however, was not part of the grand plan.

"I understand your father wrote a song called Johnny Cool" he said. Nadeeen's mum did not reply nor did her husband. They had no idea who he was talking to. It seemed as though he was either addressing the room or the wallpaper – one or the other. He certainly wasn't talking to Nadeeen because she was in the kitchen making tea.

"Anyway" he continued "Johnny Cool, I feel is an excellent song, which is my final opinion."

At this point the silence was deafening!

Nadine returned to the room with the tea and he thought "Thank Christ for that."

"My god she is lovely" he thought as he continued to stumble on. "Perhaps we could go for a drink afterwards" he said casually at which point the father "leapt forward in agreement unaware that the invitation was directed at his daughter. There was a moment of all-round hesitation.

Based on the fact that he had only met five minutes ago the response and reaction was rather odd.

The position of the young man was a tricky one but it was very good for his character. All he really wanted to do was to throw his computer and printer into the river and create with Nadeeen their very own website.

But then again life is not really like that sadly.

A MEETING WITH THE CZAR

By John Emery

He badly needed a Natasha – not any kind of Natasha but a Natasha.

He was a man who collected paintings and stamps but he also collected women too. His range ran from A for Annabelle right up to Mariella as in Frostrup.

But he was stuck on the letter N and he had an important dinner date with Roman Abramovich, the wealthy Chairman of Chelsea. So he needed some help, not only with the right girl but also with someone who could teach him Russian.

It had to be a Natasha because with a name like that she would obviously be Russian and could help him with the lingo.

This man was in a hurry. No time to stand and stare and no time to breathe he needed results and in double-quick time. One trip to the phone box solved his problem…

Natasha gives good whipping, stared at him in postcard form along with her number, "Perfect" he thought. "She is obviously Russian and collects whips, which is fine within itself."

They agreed on the phone the fee involved and he leapt into a taxi and bounded up the stairs of her Soho flat.

"Do you do Russian Natasha" he asked her. She gave him a funny look. "What do you mean?"

"Well I do a very good whipping and I could always swear at you in Russian if you like." He asked her if she was from Leningrad and she explained that she was from Balham!

He handed her an envelope containing 500 pounds and said "Forget the whipping" lets concentrate on something else.

"I want you to do something special for me." He then produced two books, War and Peace, volume one, and War and Peace, volume two.

"Natasha sit down on the bed with me"

Her eyes lit up. He fancied her after all. "Now listen I will have volume one and you have volume two, ok. You are Natasha in the book and I am Pierre Volkinov or similar. Let's get this language right. We can do it together."

"Don't you want to sleep with me then" she asked, looking beautiful in her silk lingerie. "Of course I do baby – but later."

The doorbell rang and he looked at Natasha. "He is my next customer." The next client was told to sod off.

"Listen Natasha this is big time kid. If we crack this together you will never need any more of these dreadful customers. You will live like a Queen and a Russian lady."

Natasha then intervened: "To do this correctly as from now I will call you Mr. Ivanov" he swept into raptures hugging her "Good girl- now you are getting into the swing of it."

The two of them sat on the bed trying to talk Russian for weeks with no success at all.

Then the evening came. What should they do?

"I've got it" he said and off they went to Oxford Street, he bought her a larger Russian hat – very Dr Zhivago; a £1000 fur coat and thigh gripping soft leather boots which gave her a Russian look to die for.

He had to be at the Knightsbridge home of Abramovich at 7pm and the time was tight. So into a taxi they leap and the deal was for both of them to say as little as possible.

"Just try and behave Russian and we will just busk it." They arrived ten minutes earlier at Abramovch's Knightsbridge home and were greeted by several butlers who escorted them into the lounge. Mr. Abramovich was waiting with warm greetings, "Delighted you could come. It's always nice to have a real Chelsea supporter in my home." He spoke through an interpreter.

Roman's English however was not as bad as he made out... "May I say you have a charming lady on your arm? She looks very Leningrad. May I ask her name?"

"Natasha" replied the punter who was escorted into the trophy room, of the Knightsbridge home.

He found himself in heaven at last...

There were wall to wall signed portraits of Cudicini, Melchiot, Desailles, Damien Duff, and a cast of thousands of Chelsea, past and present, a la Charlie Cooke, Peter Osgood and Huddy also known as Alan Hudson, the most under-capped player in the history of the game.

He was "lost in his dreams" for over an hour until he remembered Natasha.

He returned only to see her gliding round the room with "Mine Host" at which point he was none too pleased.

Every one today – as they say in trendy terms has a hidden agenda. His hidden agenda was the fact that he was brought up and raised in The Shed and a harder and tougher baptism to be weaned on is not possible.

He approached mine host and tapped him on the shoulder. Abramovich smiled and said, "you like my Chelsea gallery ya. Impressive don't you think." "I was just discussing with Natasha the possibility of myself taking her to a concert set in my honor next Thursday."

"She is slightly unsure as to whether she can come with me. But it's hardly a problem don't you agree? I can get you a book of season tickets for the club for the whole season."

"Listen pal" he said in true Shed-style vibrato, this girl is prettier than Mutu; quicker than Babayaro. Far more creative than Joe Cole and I assure you mate she is strictly not for sale!

The guest escorted Natasha to the exit of the lavish Knightsbridge home with Abramovich who is used to getting his own way screaming "Where are you going… Where are you going?"

Turning round casually he looked at the wealthy Abramovich and said: "I have two words to say to you and they are:

"Bugger offski."

Up, Up And Away

By John Emery

The whole procedure and difficulty of chatting up a girl in modern day London can be summed up by the activity of Victoria.

She was The Girl in the Library who everyone could talk to.

So to sweep a girl like this off her feet would surely be easy – just tell her she is lovely and adorable and then ask her out to dinner.

But on this occasion this "Easy – dating – system" had one major flaw. The guy has got to be able to see the girl before he can speak to her. So how could that be difficult?

The girl in question, Victoria, had a Spanish father who was a Magician and taught her all the tricks to enable her to avoid boring people and enthusiastic "hot blooded" young men.

You would think that the very fact that she worked in a library would be an advantage to any suitor but not in this case.

This story started when he was withdrawing a Woody Allen book.

He had not seen her before so he was caught by surprise by his own reaction. She appeared to have popped up from "Nowhere" and he would discover in time that she was equally capable of 'Disappearing just as quickly'

Perhaps she came from a circus family!

"You remind me of a girl from one of Woody Allen's films – you know the beautiful one that he always chases" he said to the slim dark haired girl in charge of the books.

"Are you Italian" he asked." "I am Spanish" she replied which was odd as she spoke fluent English.

He was in a queue, so if he wanted to achieve anything, he had to be very quick with any chat-up line that came to mind.

He continued to glare at Victoria for that was her name. He spotted it on the badge that she was wearing.

He reeled out the words, "I am seriously thinking of buying a helicopter." Beg your pardon" said Victoria.

"As I said I am seriously thinking of buying a helicopter and would like to take you away from all this. Will you come with me?"

Much to his surprise she said yes.

He couldn't believe his luck and continued to mumble and bumble as he went on his way.

He was delighted at this progress and thought "I only went in for a Woody Allen book and have ended up with a beautiful girl." He was 'very happy with this arrangement.

He looked forward to seeing her in the New Year and had great plans ready to take off in his make-believe helicopter.

But January came followed by February and there was no Victoria. He was shocked at this disappearance. Perhaps he had been seeing things.

After all he had knocked back a few beers at that time.

But all was well for she reappeared again in the month of April dressed all in white and looked sensational.

"Where have you been" he asked her. She was showing a trainee around so therefore was busy.

She had definitely progressed from any Woody Allen film she had been making and it was nice to see her again.

Prior to this he was beginning to think she might have been a "Figment of his imagination."

She appeared again two months later stamping books and much to his delight he saw this as another opportunity.

"Tell me, Victoria. Do you actually work here or not?"

She saw the joke and laughed. "Actually I am here maybe twice a week." But to add further to his confusion she added the words "I am often upstairs."

He was puzzled by this and thought what earthly reason she could have for going upstairs. The fact that it was none of his business escaped him.

He needed her to be downstairs after all so he could improve his chat up lines and impress her on a regular basis.

Then all of a sudden it came to him, the accounts department! That's what must be upstairs.

But again he really needed her to be in a visual position in the library so that every time he popped in she would be there to speak to him. Like all men he had problems with his ego!

Also he thought it was not very acceptable that this girl should drive him crazy and then disappear whenever she felt like it.

After all Victoria did say she would run away with him and a deal is a deal. She hadn't said that she had changed her mind so everything must be fine.

His very logic and powers of deduction were b "bizarre" to put it mildly.

Anyway he was seriously thinking of attaching a homing device to her body so that he could trace her dates of appearance in the library. This seemed very sensible and would be very convenient for him. He wanted to speak to her but she was making it very difficult for him.

She kept catching him by surprise.

He wished she was there when he knew she would be there. Then he could gather his suave approach work, and get it right.

The fourth meeting was a complete disaster.

He had dislocated his wrist and was wearing a bandage which he was not happy with. His typing speed vas affected but otherwise he was fine...

"What happened to your arm" she said – have you had an accident?"

He was delighted with her interest. She was obviously very concerned about his arm and cared deeply for him.

'Had you been drinking at the time' she said smiling at him as she descended the staircase.

She was doing it again! Disappearing into thin air and this time doing it before his very eyes.

This girl was making a habit of disappearing! And now she was doing it right in front of him!

Was this woman put on earth simply to taunt him and drive him crazy or what. One minute she was here and the next minute she wasn't.

He had heard of playing hard to get but this was ridiculous.

Perhaps a Magician did teach her all these tricks.

He decided to give the matter some serious thought so he decided to rent a flat opposite the library.

He then could check on her whereabouts and whether or not she was upstairs in the library or downstairs in the library.

He then bought a telescope which he attached to his window and set up a roster as to regular times of checking when and where she would arrive.

He did this for weeks with not much success and then it came to him.

"Oh my god" he thought. "She might be going in the back entrance."

He was convinced that maybe she was using the back entrance.

But what he didn't seem to work out was that he was completely obsessed with this girl, and her very beauty was driving him round the bend!

He was just about to give up when one day she stormed into the library unannounced. And by true tradition she came from out of the blue.

"Ok, lets go" she said to him. "Sorry about the delay."

He looked at her in astonishment.

She was dressed all in leather with flying goggles and boots. "Well come on then" she demanded.

"Where's the helicopter? Is it on your roof or what? I am fully aware that you live in a flat opposite and suggest we leave immediately."

They ran across the road, up the stairs and onto the roof and into the make-believe helicopter and lived happily ever after.

BIKERS GROVE
Story for Nicole

by John Emery

Nicole thought she had cracked it when biker turned up outside her office. He was dressed in leather and looked very manly.

"I'm a fool for a pretty face" he said "And you are very pretty indeed. Will you come out with me?"

Not one to hesitate, Nikki agreed.

When he had gone she began to dream if he would turn up on his 500CC Harley Davidson or not. The possibilities were endless – he might take her for a drive into the country with her sitting on the pillion; or he might take her for a wild night on the North Circular Road where she would meet all his crazy mates.

It turned out that he came by tube, and the first thing he did was to ask if he could borrow her comb.

He disappeared into the loo for 15 minutes and she began to wonder about him. She also thought she had seen the last of her comb. "Do you think I look ok" he said, having reappeared. "You look fine" she said. "Lets get a move on or we'll be late."

"Late for where?" he asked.

"Late for wherever you are taking me, that's where?" Nikki was a strong girl who knew what she wanted in life.

But here she was with a Hells Angel biker so she had nothing to worry about. On their way into the cinema he said "I couldn't borrow your mirror could I" and started to adjust him in the foyer which embarrassed Nicole." You're not gay are you" she asked directly.

"No I'm a Hells Angel, but you know that anyway…"

"It's just that you keep preening and posing like a peacock, which makes me feel a bit uncomfortable."

They went into the Cinema, one of the multiplex to see some film or other. As they sat together he produced a bottle of cologne. "Is that for me" said Nikki. "No it's mine' said the biker snatching it back. "I thought you might like to smell it. It's the latest in after shave."

She gave him another funny look.

He then began to put his arm around her but didn't seem very good at it so she helped him get a grip on the situation.

She grabbed his left arm and wrapped it firmly round her shoulder. "That's better don't you think" she said smiling.

He didn't have his bike with him but he did remember to wear his leather jacket which she liked. She began rubbing her head up against his lovely jacket.

"What are you doing" he asked Nikki. "Nothing, watch the film" she replied.

'Excuse me. This is a new jacket. Please don't rub against it. I have only just bought it."

Nikki was getting angry. Combs, mirrors, deodorants, soft leather, what on earth was she lumbered with here.

Not one to mess about she decided to put her right hand gently on his left thigh and leave it there. Now most men at this point would explode with delight.

He moved her hand away swiftly "These are my new trousers. I've only just pressed them.

The entire evening turned into an anti-climax all round. He took such a long time to work out how, when and if he was going to kiss her goodnight, she decided she couldn't hang around any more and ran off with the doorman.

After all, cinema doormen always wore such good uniforms.

Ends

GIVING IT LARGE
THE STORY OF ROSA

By John Emery

Years ago in India British troops were allocated enormous rations of a potent liquid called Rosa Rum. Anyone stationed in Delhi or otherwise would be offered what was a cross between Puccine and Scrumpy Cider. All was made up to form a very strong cocktail indeed.

This toxic brew blasted the head of many a British soldier, and was much more lethal or dangerous than the enemy.

Thus he felt it was history in the making when he met a girl of the same name in a Bayswater pub.

"Is your name really Rosa?" he asked the large lady.

She was a very big young woman and from the outset all he wanted to do was bury him inside her ample body. Her curves knocked him bandy and he told her that he loved big women.

He licked his lips as he surveyed her generous frame and felt that he could occasionally pop up for air while making love to her but only if absolutely necessary.

"I really go for large women" he kept telling her as though he was doing her a favor. He shouldn't have done this for she quite liked him.

"Ok" she said "Will you buy me dinner."

"Of course," he replied behaving like the perfect gentleman. He agreed and she ordered steak and chips twice and a large cheesecake, covered in whipped cream and washed down with three bottles of wine.

He looked on with glee as she scoffed through the food, whipped cream and wine. She devoured them as though there was no tomorrow.

His sole intention was to devour her in exactly the same way.

"Any way as I was saying" he said to her "I don't really like slim girls at all."

"Really" she said. "No I prefer large girls like you. Would you like me to tell you a story?"

It was based on the fact that Clockwork Orange writer Anthony Burgess, had once slept with a model and declared that he was "cut to pieces" by her sharp elbows and sharp knees.

He burst out laughing as Rosa looked on. "What's the point of the story then" she asked.

"Oh simple, Burgess was saying that slim models were hopeless and that he always preferred his women to be big."

"Did he really," smiled Rosa. She wiped the plate clean and proceeding to order two more helpings of cheesecake covered in cream. He was in his element watching all of this happen.

He sat dreaming of the "Night in heaven" that lay ahead for him. The very prospect of cuddling up to this woman drove him wild with desire.

She put her hand on his knee and whispered in his ear, "are you a gambling man?" and he smiled in the direction of yes...

"Well how about some fun then?"

She suggested that they play snooker against each other but with the added incentive of it being strip snooker.

Every time a player pots a ball the other removes a garment. They were the rules. This seemed quite a tame idea except for the fact that it was to be played in front of a pub packed full of people.

He cunningly held back the fact that he was champion of Pool at his local club.

He decided to break and the first shot he potted was a red followed by a green.

Rosa removed first her watch and then her necklace. He reminded Rosa that she was supposed to remove her clothing not other items.

"Down boy" she said to him. "Be patient. All will come to those who wait."

It was her go and she proceeded to pot a red, then a green, then a red, then a black, then a red, then a blue.

She eventually cleaned up – yet again – by potting every colour, leaving him standing stark naked in front of a packed pub. He looked very silly standing there with no clothes on.

She walked up to him, kissed him warmly on the cheek and said clearly, " that will teach you. No one ever calls me fat."

She left the pub to a standing ovation.

FLOWER ARRANGING

By John Emery

There is an old Rod Stewart song titled "A dirty old raincoat will never let you down" but in this case it was bad advice… he walked into room with all the right ingredients, blond hair, good dress sense…

At first glance she knew he would be the right choice. The word that came to mind was compact. He was slick and beefy – not big & ugly which seemed to be the new mode of the Neanderthal man.

"Big may be the new mode" she twittered to her petite friend. "But I do not want some great lump on top me thank you very much." Her petite friend smiled.

De Lalleo may be captain of the England rugby team but he is not every woman's dream as the magazines may have you imagine. The young lady in question was more interested in something more compact in size…

Someone to grab hold of firmly in the midriff, as she decided to give away her most precious possession of all – her virginity.

The young lady was of such age that she needed to be deflowered. This had nothing to do with flower arranging as such. But nevertheless it was something that had to be done. Her dad always told her that whatever she did – to do it properly or not at all.

If a young lady decided that she wanted to give away her most precious possession then the "Lucky Guy" had to be very special, otherwise what was the point, but the decision had been made.

The final countdown was upon us; we were about to have lift off; and indeed she did expect the earth to move.

And rightly so. If not she could always ask for her money back!

She looked him up and down assessing the goods and agreed he was top quality hetero material.

But hold on… where did he get that raincoat?

A young lady could not be seen with a man in a grubby raincoat – it just wasn't done. "You cannot walk about in a raincoat like that," she told him candidly. "And why not," he said.

Take a good look at what you see was the message signaled to him. In other words it was either her or the raincoat. One of them had to go.

He sold the raincoat the next day.

Taming Of The Shrew
The Story Of Katie

By John Emery

Hell hath no fury like a woman scorned is a good old William Shakespeare phrase. And so it was with Katie. The fact that she had the same name as the woman featured in the taming of the shrew was pure irony.

Katie was a girl with gumption but there again she had to be. Her boyfriend was a musician and they do not even know how to spell the word, monogamy. Let alone put it into practice.

But she always stood her ground and fought off all-comers who seemed to be popping up everywhere from day one. "Who are these girls anyway" Katie would say.

"They are my fans" the musician would say.

"Well get rid of them or I will."

He totally ignored her. But then that's what most men do – ignore women so there is nothing new there.

Her day was about to come however with the appearance of Henrietta De Arc – a pencil – slim blonde, who had a name to match her designer clothing. She arrived with a shoulder bag; shades; a bag full of credit cards and confidence to match.

"Hi my name is Henrietta. You can just call be Harry – everybody else does.

She clicked her fingers on arrival.

"Large glass of white wine please and a pint of larger will do nicely" Her fingers "clicked" in the direction of Katie who she thought was the waitress.

She addressed the musician in a direct but cuddly manner, I understand you are looking for a girl singer and I have to be the one. Don't you agree? "I don't know" said the musician. "Can you sing?"

"Sing – of course I can sing" said Henrietta. "But you must agree I definitely look the part."

The musician nodded. "You do look the part indeed. I agree. But can you sing?" She nodded again. "Well give me a song then."

She blushed. "I can't sing in here. It's a pub. I would be happy to sing in rehearsal with you in front of a proper band."

Katie was beginning to get angry.

Who did this woman think she was anyway, just walking in and trying to take her boyfriend away? But the musician/boyfriend was nobody's fool.

"Do you like the early stuff of Elkie Brooks – the time she spent along Robert Palmer with a band called Vinegar Joe… How about Etta James, Bessie Smith, and the early work of Ike and Tina Turner?

Henrietta looked confused "I was thinking more along the lines of-Geri Halliwell, Billie Piper, Dido and Madonna."

"We don't do that" said the musician. "We play proper music here and are looking for a gutsy singer with passion who can stay the pace. You are not the one we are looking for."

Henrietta started banging on the table like a spoilt child so much so that he had no choice but to grab her firmly, put her over his knee and spank her in a fatherly manner.

"Now go home like a good little girl, practice for two years, give my regards to your dad then ring me then and not before."

Having smacked her bottom he escorted her to the door marked exit. Katie stood in the background knowing yet again that another contender for her title had come and gone within the space of ten minutes – without her having to even lift an eyebrow.

Blonde On Blonde

By John Emery

If Emmylou had looked like Marvin Gaye she could have been tagged a Stubborn Kinda Fella. But being Blonde on Blonde. Swedish and 100% female the only thing they had in common was the word stubborn.

She arrived in London from Stockholm, and was an immediate hit with everyone, but found the English Language very difficult. So she decided early on to contrive her very own style of communication. It was deliberate and it was effective.

She was very beautiful and had her fair share of admirers. Will you come to dinner with me next week, it's my birthday, would be a normal invitation.

"No," she would reply and simply walk casually away. But instead of annoying her admirers they lapped it up and would come back for more. She had such a sensuous way of saying the "No" everyone loved her for it.

Her admirers would queue up and invite her out to cinemas, theatres, dinners, parties, holidays and the answer would always be "No."

But the more she would say no the more they would keep trying. They would goad her and even deliberately annoy her just so that she would say the magic word.

Emmylou's vocabulary was not as limited as people thought, however. She had two words that she would use-the other one was ok.

The one thing that annoyed her however was her name. It was not Swedish. It was not English and didn't seem to make any sense at all.

The reason behind it was that her mother loved country music and named her after Emmylou Harris who was a big country success in the States.

But her decision to limit her vocabulary to two words worked like a dream. Everyone loved her.

But it was also used cleverly as a "cover" for what was a very stubborn personality.

A handsome guy would ask her to come out with him. If the answer was no, that was her final decision.

She would sometimes say ok and go to the pictures but only when she felt like it.

Emmylou, however, was very bright indeed. She simply enjoyed giving the impression that she was a bit stupid just to drive the men wild.

It worked when she was a pretty young girl so she decided to carry it forward. After all why change a winning formula.

She broke a lot of hearts along the way but even when she said no she always said it with a smile.

Emmylou was firm and stubborn and would never budge. But eventually her little vocabulary began to backfire on her and word spread around. "There is a Swedish girl who will say no to you in such a way that you will have an orgasm in your trousers. It's just the way she says it."

"Please" an admirer would say "Let me kiss you" no she would reply. This would drive him wild and he would come back again and again.

One admirer decided to bombard her with presents considering it an honor if she simply accepted them. "Did you like that dress I sent to you last week?" She would say ok. "Did you receive the chocolates as well?"

The answer was not ok but she smiled for she knew he was trying to wind her up.

When she smiled she looked like the Mona Lisa. It seemed to open up her heart and he could see right inside her very character.

On a clear day you could catch her at a certain angle and under a certain light she was absolutely beautiful. She didn't need any make-up.

That was another thing she didn't bother with.

Make up and words. They were both a waste of time and things that she did not need.

But what about a man – surely she would need one of them. "Ok she would smile, but only when I am ready." The last time he saw Emmylou there was a queue a mile long outside her bar applying for the vacant post of Male Escort. She was interviewing each one in a casual manner.

He could see her turning them away one by one in her own dismissive style.

And in his ear he could hear the magic word NO, many, many times.

A Badge Called Kelly

By John Emery

There was a young lady called Shelley whose name at work was Kelly which made life very confusing.

On a daily basis he would walk into his bank where she worked and nonchalantly say "Hi Kelly" at which point she would scream at him," Don't ever call me Kelly. My name is Shelley."

This always made him jump.

But the fault lay with the bank because they had her badge printed up as Kelly whereupon her name was Shelley.

It was a simple mistake but one that was about to change his entire life for he had every intention of chasing this girl from the fist day she arrived at the bank.

Every time he tried to do it however he got her name wrong so just like snakes and ladders he had to go all the way back to the beginning and start again.

However he was very determined and there was no way a silly little badge was going to put him off.

In his spare time he would rehearse his chat up lines to get them right. He would say to himself "Remember her name is Shelley. Just ignore the badge."

So his new plan was to keep it simple and just stick to the word HELLO.

Having decided this he made his first move.

"Excuse me – would you like to come out to dinner one evening."

She looked back at him and said, I have a name you know and if you want to take me out to dinner surely you can do it properly by asking me nicely.

But I have asked you nicely he pointed out. "I just can't get your name right."

"Yes" she replied "But that's your problem isn't it. It's got nothing to do with me and she casually walked away.

He really fancied her and decided to "Jump in at the deep end" so the next time he saw her he grabbed her by the shoulders and said "Why won't you come out with me?"

At this point she called the Manager.

"This man is assaulting me. Have him removed."

He was taken to the manger's office, given a severe reprimand and told that if this incident happened again his Credit Card would have to be returned, his account with the bank would be closed and his £30,000 overdraft would be called in immediately.

He couldn't believe this.

All he did was try and ask a girl out to dinner and was on the verge of total ruin.

So he decided that the only thing to do was murder her. He had no choice.

He worked out that it was best to do it one evening when she was on her own.

So on a Friday evening at the end of the week he waited in a doorway as planned. As she passed by he pulled her into the doorway trying to grab her neck in a vice like grip.

He squeezed her neck very hard indeed.

She was not surprised or shocked at all. She knew exactly who it was.

"What are you doing hiding in a doorway you idiot? Are you trying to murder me?"

"Yes I am actually," he confirmed. "Now will you please keep still?"

He forced his grip round her neck in the doorway and then realized what he was doing. "I am physically assaulting a really nice girl in a doorway"

"I had no idea that you felt this way," said Shelley. So why don't we pop down the road for dinner and discuss this matter sensible."

He paused for a minute and agreed.

"But there is one condition," he said with great authority, - that you give me your badge."

"Ok if you insist".

He then proceeded to throw the badge as far away as possible.

"Do you realize that thing nearly ruined a beautiful relationship?"

They were last seen wandering off, hand in hand, chatting happily about Spaghetti Bolognaise.

And they never saw the badge again!!!

Horace

By John Emery

She was a little late for her date so put the skids on her legs in a desperate attempt to get her to the church on time. Christine had always had trouble with men the trouble being that she couldn't get one.

She tried everything to pull a bloke but had no luck.

To approach a dating agency was against everything she believed in but she had no choice. She was supposed to meet him under the clock at the station at 7 pm and she was running late. Christine was actually physically running late to the date and was a bit of a clown so the odds of her skidding and falling over, was very much on the cards.

But she got there on time and there he was. Dark hair, 5 foot 10 and a red carnation in his button hole as instructed by the agency.

Christine was very impressed and thought that it might be a mistake. "Are you sure you are from the dating agency." He smiled and nodded in the direction of yes.

He was a stunningly handsome man and very well dressed and looked a bit like Kevin Costner on his day off.

Surely she thought that the last thing this guy would ever need was any help at all in finding a girlfriend.

They handed each other a card from the agency and adjourned to a Starbucks for coffee. They spoke over coffee and croissants and Christine was convinced there had to be a catch somewhere with this character for her date was not only handsome but also very charming.

She did have a point for the "catch" so to speak was just about to arrive in the shape of his name.

"My name is Horace," he said offering to shake her hand. "Horace Morris, actually."

Strange name for a guy who looked like a matinee idol but there you go. Perhaps he was joking. Actually he wasn't joking at all but it didn't really matter. The catch so to speak was his background.

Horace was the son of Boris and Doris Morris, who were without question the worse double act ever to appear on stage. They did the circuit for years with an act so awful it had to be seen to be believed. Boris and Doris however had no idea that they were that bad because they were constantly booked.

"Its Boris and Doris Morris" was the introduction as the two jumped onto the stage with verve and enthusiasm. They had a sequence of jokes and a set pattern for their act which would always end with their own catchphrase. "Is that funny or whaaat!!!" At which point the audience would reply. No.

Boris Moris would say "Our future is with our son Horace Moris. He will knock 'em bandy. He will be so funny he will destroy the audience with just one glance in their direction."

But the one thing that they could not foresee was that they were about to give birth to a son who was to develop into probably the most handsome young man in the history of life itself.

He was so good looking that girls would faint in his very presence. They would see him on the Central Line and physically pass out.

It didn't take long before Horace got well fed up with this. "All they want is romance and all I want to do is make people laugh"

By the age of 22 Horace actually looked like a cross between Tom Cruise and Keanu Reeves and decided to go the agency.

He desperately wanted a girl who could accept all this and not keep going all romantic on him. Whether Christine was the right one only time would tell.

The first evening went quite well until they had to say goodbye. Christine snuggled up to Horace who whispered in her ear "Would you like to smell my carnation."

"How romantic he is" she thought moving her pert little face towards the flower. The next thing she knew she was covered in water for it turned out to be a joke flower!!

Horace jumped back with delight hollering "Is that funny or whaaat" and began to laugh incessantly. Christine was mortified.

She stood outside her house in designer clothes covered in water. She was horrified at this man's behavior and slapped him round the face with such a clout; you could hear it in the next road.

"Are you mad or what – I thought you were a nice guy."

Horace jumped to his own defense. "I was only joking. Would you like to see my water pistol instead?" He then produced an enormous blue plastic contraption from his other pocket and proceeded to squirt her with more water!!!

"Is that funny or whaaat" Horace again squealed with delight. Christine had no idea that her first date could end in such a disaster.

"First you squeeze your carnation at me and then follow it by trying to drown me with a water pistol. What's the matter with you?"

"I'm a comedian." said Horace. "One day I will be famous" "Is there any chance that you will see me again."

Christine looked at him slowly assessing the situation. This guy was Drop Dead Gorgeous but was obviously seriously insane! "Listen Horace" she said "I will do a deal with you. Don't use your water pistol on me any more and I will see you again. Also I want a proper kiss from you before I go to bed."

He proceeded to kiss her and it had such an effect that she became weak at the knees.

She did see him again and continued to but it cost her, a fortune in dry cleaning bills!

About the Authors

JOHN EMERY is a writer with a great deal of experience in Rock Music having worked for Beat Instrumental, Beatles Monthly, National rockstar and as Press Officer for Jimmy James & The Vagabonds and the Steve Gibbons Band. His basis training was in Fleet Street with the Press Association, the Evening Standard and the Daily Mail.

Recently he completed his first musical ONE EUROPE and he is currently working on the second book of short stories.

****

JEFF MARKHAM can be described as one of the "New Wave" of artists with something fresh and exciting to offer. His work is oil inspired and can be categorised simply as a Modern Art at its best.

His entry into Art was slightly delayed and followed a long period establishing himself as a Corporate Accountant with a large International Bank in the City.

His influences include Roy Lichtenstein, Jackson Pollock, Francis Bacon and a wide range of painters, who after a lot of hard work created a style of his very own.

Lightning Source UK Ltd.
Milton Keynes UK
10 March 2010

151220UK00001B/44/A